BERNARD WABER

Funny, Funny Lyle

Houghton Mifflin Company Boston

for my grandson
Mason

Library of Congress Cataloging-in-Publication Data

Waber, Bernard.
    Funny, Funny Lyle.

    Summary: Lyle the crocodile experiences many changes
in his life when his mother moves in with the Primm
family and Mrs. Primm announces she is expecting a baby.
    [1. Crocodiles—Fiction] I. Title.
PZ7.W113Fu 1987   [E]   86-27772
ISBN 0-395-43619-2
PAP ISBN 0-395-60287-4

Printed in Mexico

WOZ 10 9 8 7 6

Swish! Swash! Splash! Swoosh!
Strange sounds come from
the house on East 88th Street.
Can it be Lyle, Lyle the Crocodile,
enjoying his bath?

Actually not — not this time.
This time it is Lyle's mother —
and having a good bath at that.

Soaking in a tub of sudsy rainbow bubbles is by far her greatest pleasure.

Although she has only just arrived
from the land of the crocodile,
Lyle's mother is already very much
at home living with Mr. and Mrs. Primm,
their son, Joshua, and Lyle.
Especially Lyle.

She is on the happiest
of terms with Bird.

And she enjoys
good, long visits
with Loretta,
the cat next door.

And now she even has a name — Felicity.
"It's so awkward always having to speak of her
as 'Lyle's mother'," Mrs. Primm remarked one day.
"She needs to have her own name."
Everyone began suggesting names.
Joshua suggested Tabatha. But Lyle's mother
made a face when she heard Tabatha.
"How about Nile?" said Mr. Primm.
"Nile?" said Mrs. Primm.
"As in Nile the Crocodile," said Mr. Primm.
Lyle's mother made another face,
a really scornful face this time.

"How about Felicity?" said Mrs. Primm.
"It means happiness, and certainly she has
brought only happiness to this house."
Lyle's mother smiled — a big, big smile.
She even did a handstand to show her approval.
"She likes it!" everyone cried out at once.
"Then Felicity it must be," said Mr. Primm.
And so, from that day, Lyle's mother was
called Felicity, a name of her own choosing.

But to Lyle she could only be mother.
Mother — the very sound of the word filled
him with joy. Lyle was so proud of his
mother. He was proud of her beauty . . .

and her enormous talent for making everyone
smile and feel merry wherever she went.

Lyle especially liked the hours he spent
alone with his mother when Mr. and Mrs. Primm
were away at work, and Joshua at school —
just the two of them doing chores.
Lyle always washed the breakfast dishes.
He rubbed and he scrubbed and he dipped
and he splashed.
Felicity cared for the plants, and arranged
fresh guest towels. She always favored ones
with bright, colorful flowered prints.

And together they waited
for Joshua to return from school,
so they all could play until dark.

Oh, the world
was a wonderful place,
thought Lyle. And he couldn't
think of anything he
wanted changed.

Still, changes were taking place.
For one thing, several new locks were necessary
now to safeguard the house.
And a sign in the window read: BEWARE OF CROCODILES.
"You can't be too careful," Mr. Primm said, shaking
his head sadly.

Lyle wondered what he would do
if a robber broke into the house.
He practiced making mean, ferocious faces.

He growled

and he scowled

and he snarled

and he hissed

and he scared himself
half to death.

But there were other, more happy changes.
"Felicity, Lyle, I have something most important
to tell both of you," said Mrs. Primm, one day.
Everyone sat down. Mrs. Primm smoothed her skirt
as she gathered her thoughts.
"Well," she began at last, "what do you suppose
will be happening around here?"
Lyle stared at Mrs. Primm and could not suppose
whatever it was he was supposed to be supposing.
Mrs. Primm began again. "I . . . I mean we . . . well
actually all of us, dears, we're going to have. . . ."
A robbery! thought Lyle, his eyes widening.
"A baby," said Mrs. Primm. "Aren't you surprised?"
They shook their heads yes, and were indeed
surprised. Very surprised.

"Isn't it wonderful!" Mrs. Primm exclaimed,
throwing her arms around Lyle and his mother,
and rocking back and forth with them.
"Oh, Felicity and Lyle," she cried, "I know
you both will be so much help when
the baby arrives."

Lyle was surprised all right.
For the next several days, all he could
think about was the baby.
He tried to picture the Primm's baby
— and himself taking care of it.
He would walk the baby — proudly.

And he would feed the baby, too.

And babysit.

And he would comfort the baby if it cried.
This is what he would do if the baby cried:
He would cradle the baby in his arms, and gently
rock it, and coo to it, and make silly faces,
silly, silly crocodile faces, until the baby would
laugh and be happy again. Lyle smiled just
thinking about it, and now could hardly wait
for the baby to be born.

Months went by as preparations for the baby's arrival moved cheerily along. Everyone helped paint the nursery. Because he was tallest, Lyle did the ceiling.

And there was shopping to do.
One day, Mrs. Primm, Felicity, and Lyle
went to a big store to buy clothes for the baby.

Felicity, who had never been to a store,
was immediately drawn to the perfumes.
Poof! Poof! She joyously sprayed herself.
Poof! Poof! She went eagerly from bottle to bottle.
Mrs. Primm and Lyle could hardly coax her away.

Finally, they did coax her, and were about to
leave the store when suddenly everyone was
surprised to hear angry voices scream out,
"STOP! STOP, THIEF!"
And just as suddenly, they were even more
surprised to see two men race up to Felicity
and rip apart her shopping bag.

Out tumbled bottle after bottle
of perfume and cologne.
"Madam!" shouted one of the men. "This is
stolen property. You are under arrest!"
"Oh, Felicity," cried Mrs. Primm.

Felicity could not understand what was happening.
She thought the men rude, and needful of
lessons in good manners. She began swatting
at them with her purse.
Thereupon, the men leaped on Felicity.
Lyle rushed to her rescue, and everyone tossed,
tussled, and tangled all over the floor.

Soon after, the police arrived.
Mrs. Primm and Lyle stood helplessly by
as Felicity was hustled away . . .

first, to be fingerprinted, and then photographed, and finally locked up for the night.

And all through that long and difficult night,
no one in the house slept. The entire family stayed
awake, fretting about and dearly missing Felicity
— especially Lyle.

The next morning, Felicity stood before a judge.
"So, Felicity," said the judge, "you have broken the
law, and now you must pay for your crime."
"Please, judge," said Mrs. Primm. "Felicity is new
to our ways. She wouldn't know about stealing."

"Well then," said the judge, "so that she will
learn the difference between the good life
and the bad, I sentence Felicity to no less than
six months of work — work of her own choosing,
that must serve the needs of others."

Felicity chose to help out at the hospital.
Although he admired how well his mother looked in
her new, crisp uniform, Lyle was sad watching her leave
for work each morning with Mr. and Mrs. Primm.

Felicity soon decided she liked, and would
continue, to work — work she was superb at doing.
And yet she, too, was saddened;
saddened all the long day, away from her son.
But what was a mother to do?
One day, Lyle accompanied Felicity to her job.
When he saw how expertly she cared for her patients,
Lyle was never more proud of his mother.
And he spent the rest of the day helping her.

In time, Lyle almost got used to his mother's absence. Each day, he looked forward to playing with Joshua and their friends.

And there was something else to look forward to —
a most exciting, most wonderful something: The birth
of the baby — although it seemed to Lyle the baby
was taking its good, sweet time getting on with the
business of being born.

One night Lyle woke up with a start.
He was certain he heard footsteps on the stairs.
And suddenly, he was even more certain those
very same footsteps belonged to robbers.
Robbers in the house!

Lyle knew exactly what to do.
Bravely, he put on his most ferocious face,
and prepared to battle the robbers.
He even surprised himself, he was so brave.
He huffed . . . and he puffed . . .
and he flung himself out the door.
And . . .

almost fell upon Mr. and Mrs. Primm and Felicity.
"Lyle," said Mrs. Primm, "we were just coming to tell you it is time, time for the baby to be born."
"And how good to have our own Nurse Felicity go with us to the hospital," said Mr. Primm.